Learning to Read and Write Step by Step!

Ready to Read and Write Preschool–Kindergarten
• big type and easy words
• picture clues
• drawing and first writing activities

For children who like to "tell" stories by drawing pictures and are eager to write.

Reading and Writing with Help Preschool–Grade 1
• basic vocabulary
• short sentences
• simple writing activities

For children who use letters, words, and pictures to tell stories.

Reading and Writing on Your Own Grades 1–3
• popular topics
• easy-to-follow plots
• creative writing activities

For children who are comfortable writing simple sentences on their own.

STEP INTO READING® Write-In Readers are designed to give every child a successful reading and writing experience. The grade levels are only guides. Children can progress through the steps at their own speed, developing confidence in their abilities, no matter what grade.

Remember, a lifetime love of reading and writing starts with a single step!

Thomas the Tank Engine & Friends®

A BRITT ALLCROFT COMPANY PRODUCTION

Based on The Railway Series by The Reverend W Awdry
Copyright © 2006 Gullane (Thomas) LLC
Thomas the Tank Engine & Friends and Thomas & Friends are trademarks of
Gullane Entertainment Inc.
Thomas the Tank Engine & Friends is Reg. U.S. Pat. TM Off.

A HIT Entertainment Company

www.stepintoreading.com
www.thomasandfriends.com

Educators and librarians, for a variety of teaching tools, visit us at
www.randomhouse.com/teachers

ISBN-13: 978-0-375-83464-6
ISBN-10: 0-375-83464-8
Library of Congress Control Number: 2005931975
Printed in the United States of America
10 9 8 7 6 5 4 3 2 1 First Edition

STEP INTO READING

STEP **2**

Henry's Bad Day

A Write-In Reader

Based on *The Railway Series* by the Rev. W. Awdry

and

_____

Illustrated by Richard Courtney and

_____

Random House 🏠 New York

Henry loves
his bright green paint.
It is clean and shiny.

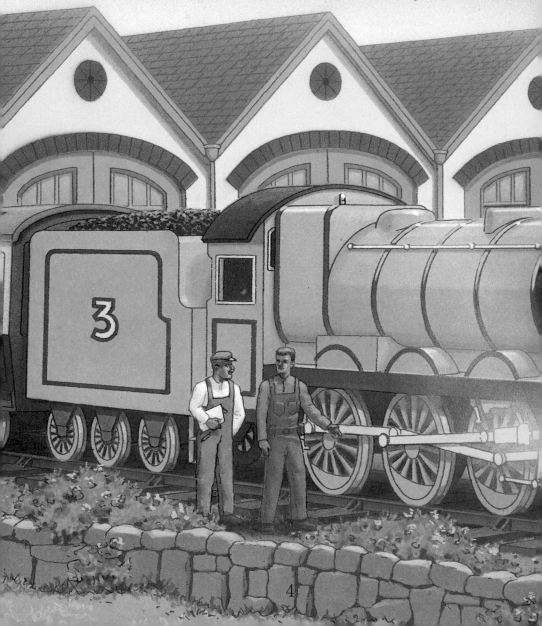

On sunny days,
Henry sparkles.

"Gordon,"
said Henry,
"see how handsome I am."
"Wheesht!"
snorted Gordon.
"You are not handsome.
You are vain."

How would you describe Henry?

On rainy days,
Henry is cross.
Rain makes spots
on his shiny coat.

How do you feel when it is rainy?

Draw yourself.

_____

_ _ _ _ _ _ _ _ _ _ _

_____

One rainy day,
Henry's coaches
were full.
He was going fast.

Henry saw a tunnel.

The tunnel was dry.

Henry stopped
inside the dry tunnel.

The passengers
did not want to stop.
They wanted to go.
Henry would not go.

The passengers pushed.

The passengers pulled.

Henry would not go.

Sir Topham Hatt was mad.
"You must go!" he said.
Henry would not go.

Sir Topham Hatt called the workmen.

The passengers got on
Bertie the Bus.

The workmen made a wall
in front of Henry.

Henry was glad to be dry.

Write the names
of these things
that you can build with.

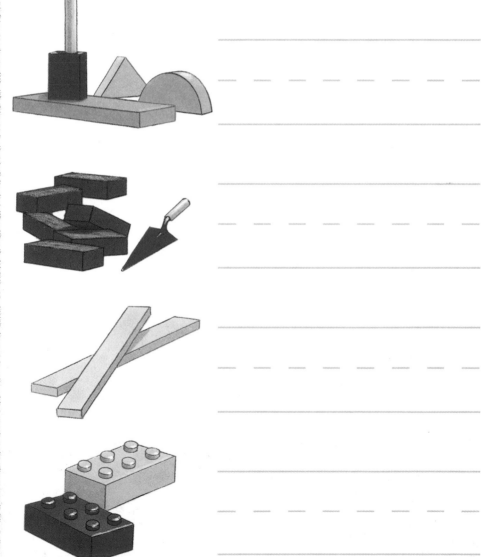

Many weeks went by.

Henry was bored.

Henry was lonely.

Henry saw Gordon go by.

What do you do
when you are bored?
Draw it.

One day,
Gordon was pulling
the Express.
It broke down near Henry.

Pretend you are on the Express. Write to a friend.

Dear ________________________,
(your best friend)

I am on the Express. I am going to ________________________.
(a place)

My favorite engine is ________________________.
(an engine)

The train just stopped. This is what I think the reason is:
________________________.

See you soon, ________________________
(your name)

Who can help?

Edward is too small.

James is too far away.

"I am sorry.
I was silly,"
peeped Henry.
"I can help."

The workmen opened
the tunnel.
Henry was dirty.
But he was happy
to be going.

He pushed the Express.
Slowly, slowly, slowly,
the Express moved.

Henry pushed harder.
Faster and faster
they all moved.

Soon they saw
the station.

Sir Topham Hatt
thanked Henry for being
a Really Useful Engine.

What will they use to clean Henry up?

Henry is
no longer vain.
But he still
hates the rain.